W9-CSD-530

Let's Fix It!

DORA
the explorer

publications international, ltd.

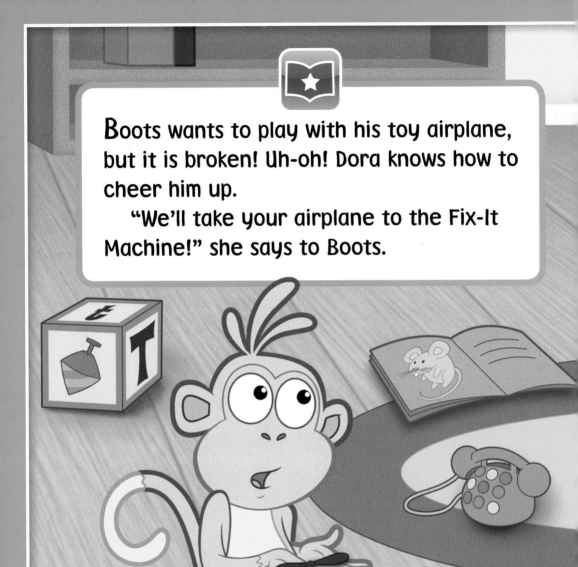

Boots wants to play with his toy airplane, but it is broken! Uh-oh! Dora knows how to cheer him up.

"We'll take your airplane to the Fix-It Machine!" she says to Boots.

Dora and Boots check the Map. Map tells them to go past Isa's Garden and through Spooky Forest, and that's how they'll get to the Fix-It Machine.

Dora and Boots make it to Isa's Garden! But Isa isn't gardening. She says that her garden shovel is broken. Dora has an idea.

"We can take your shovel to the Fix-It Machine, too!" she tells Isa.

The friends go to Spooky Forest.
When they arrive, Tico offers them
a ride on his bicycle.

The forest is very dark. Dora finds something in Backpack that will help her, Boots, and Tico see where they are going. It's a flashlight!

On the other side of Spooky Forest, the friends find Benny. Benny is upset because his guitar has a broken string.

"Don't worry, Benny," Dora says. "We're going to the Fix-It Machine. We'll take your guitar!"

Dora and Boots make it to the Fix-It Machine. Uh-oh! Swiper is coming! Does he want to swipe the Fix-it Machine?

The friends need to stop Swiper. They say, "Swiper, no swiping! Swiper, no swiping! Swiper, no swiping!" But Swiper wasn't trying to swipe the Fix-it Machine. He just needs something fixed, too — his yo-yo!

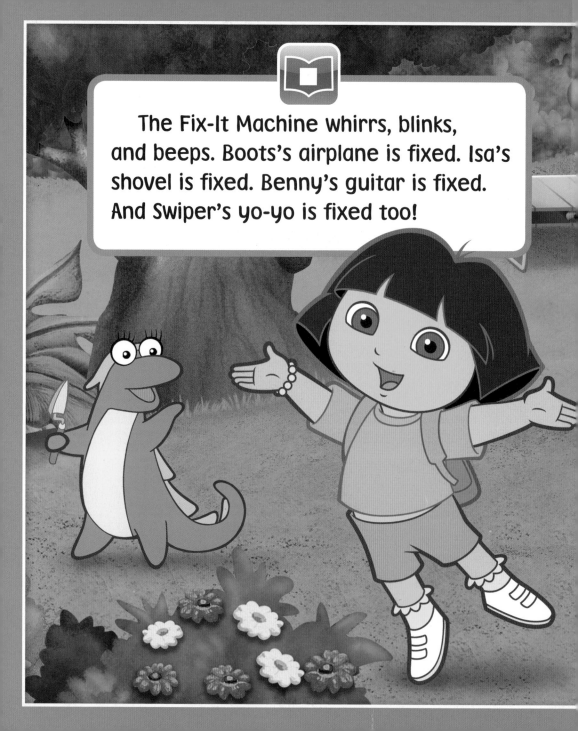

The Fix-It Machine whirrs, blinks, and beeps. Boots's airplane is fixed. Isa's shovel is fixed. Benny's guitar is fixed. And Swiper's yo-yo is fixed too!

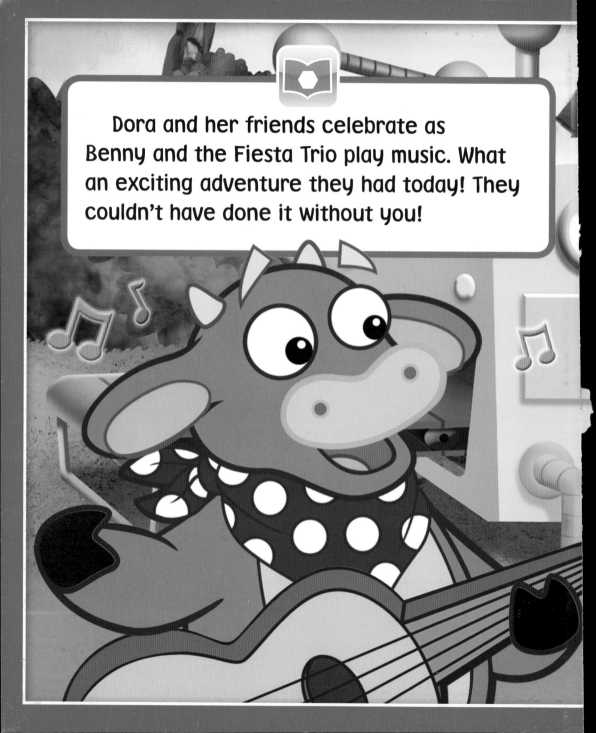

Dora and her friends celebrate as Benny and the Fiesta Trio play music. What an exciting adventure they had today! They couldn't have done it without you!